Everybody Feels...
SAD!

Moira Butterfield & Holly Sterling

Consultant: Cecilia Essau
Design: Barbi Sido, Mike Henson
Editor: Carly Madden
Editorial Director: Victoria Garrard
Art Director: Laura Roberts-Jensen
Associate Publisher: Maxime Boucknooghe
Publisher: Zeta Jones

First published in the UK in 2016 by
QED Publishing
Part of The Quarto Group
The Old Brewery
6 Blundell Street
London N7 9BH

www.qed-publishing.co.uk

A catalogue record for this book is
available from the British Library.

ISBN 978 1 78493 425 5

Printed in China

Contents

Feeling sad!

Everybody feels sad sometimes. You might get sad if...

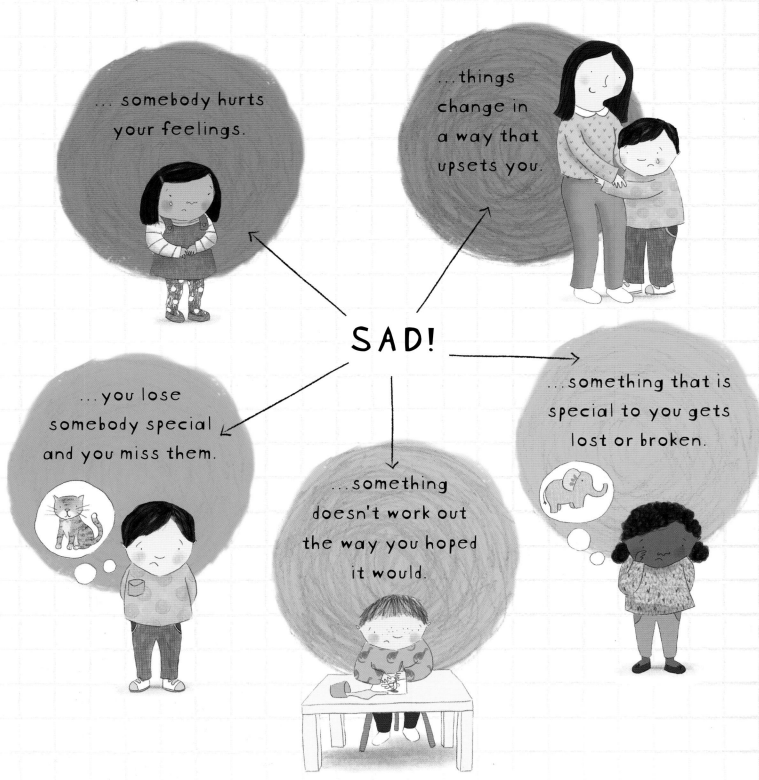

... somebody hurts your feelings.

...things change in a way that upsets you.

SAD!

...you lose somebody special and you miss them.

...something doesn't work out the way you hoped it would.

...something that is special to you gets lost or broken.

How it feels

Are your eyes filled with tears?

Has your smile disappeared?

Does your heart feel

like a heavy weight?

Have you lost your laugh?

Do you want to hide?

You must be feeling...

Sad!

Sad girl

Hello. I'm Chloe. One day I lost my little toy elephant Beebee.

Beebee, where are you?

I searched everywhere at home, but I couldn't find her.

That night I didn't have Beebee to put under my pillow.

I really missed my favourite toy.

The next morning I couldn't
put Beebee in my school bag
like I always did.

She wasn't going to
be with me anymore.

Thinking about it made
me cry, so Mum gave
me a hug.

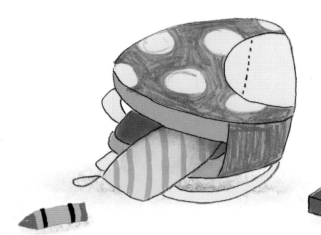

At playtime I didn't feel like joining in. It's hard to play when you're feeling sad.

My friends saw my sad face and asked me what was wrong.

Are you OK, Chloe?

I told my friends
why **I** was so upset.

They said they
would help me
look for Beebee
around school.

We'll help!

Guess what? Sophie found Beebee
in the corner of the playground!

Woohoo! Thanks, Sophie.

Straight away I went
from sadness to happiness.
I felt much better!

Sad boy

Hello. My name's Omar. I once had a lovely, cuddly cat called Socks.

She had soft grey fur with fluffy white feet, and I loved her very much.

One day Dad had to take Socks to the vet because she was ill.

When he came home he told us that poor Socks had died.

I felt very upset, as if a big blanket of sadness was wrapped all around me.

I wished and wished that I could bring Socks back, but I couldn't.

Then Mum and Dad sat down with me and we talked about Socks.

We remembered how she rubbed around our legs and purred.

14

We looked at some photos of Socks and we remembered how much she loved to have outdoor adventures.

A little while after Socks died, Mum took
me round to my friend Ethan's house.

He had a cat called Snowball, and she had two kittens.
They had fluffy white feet, just like my old cat Socks.

The kittens came to live with us.
I called them Mops and Meg.

I still remembered Socks,
but I began to feel less sad.

I was too busy looking after
Mops and Meg to feel sad!

Feeling better

Chloe felt sad when she lost her favourite toy.

When she told her friends, they helped her to find it. Then the feeling of sadness disappeared.

18

When Omar's cat Socks died, he was very sad.

He began to feel better when he talked about Socks's happy life and then became busy looking after his new kittens.

Chloe's story

1 Chloe lost her toy elephant Beebee.

2 Beebee was like a little friend to Chloe, so she felt upset.

3 Chloe shared her feelings with her friends, and they helped her.

4 Chloe's sadness quickly turned to happiness when Beebee was found.

20

Omar's story

1 Omar's pet cat Socks died, and he missed her.

2 He remembered happy times with Socks.

3 Omar got two new kittens.

4 Though he would always love Socks, he began to feel less upset.

Story words

blanket
A big piece of thick warm material that wraps around you. Omar felt as if he was covered in a blanket of sadness when Socks died.

busy
Having lots to do. Being busy helped Omar feel less sad.

favourite
Something that you like very much, more than anything else. Beebee was Chloe's favourite toy.

fluffy
Fuzzy and soft. Omar remembered that Socks's feet were fluffy.

remembered
When you have thought about things that happened to you in the past. Omar remembered happy times with Socks.

shared
When something is given to another person. Chloe shared her feelings with her friends by telling them about Beebee.

special
Something that is different to everything else. Beebee was a special toy for Chloe.

upset
When someone feels unhappy.

vet
Somebody who looks after sick animals.

weight
Something heavy. When people are sad they sometimes say their heart feels heavy.

Next steps

The stories in this book have been written to give children an introduction to feeling sad through events that they are familiar with. Here are some ideas to help you explore the feelings from the story together.

Talking

- Look at Chloe and Omar's stories. Talk about what made them both sad. How did it feel to be sad?

- Ask your child if they can remember a time when they felt sad, and why. Think about how good memories helped Omar feel less sad after his pet died.
- Discuss how Chloe told her friends her feelings, and how it helped her. Talk about why it's good to tell somebody when you feel sad.
- Look at page 11 – point out how sad feelings can go away quickly if things change. Can the children think of any examples of this?
- Read the poem on page 5 together and talk to your child about how they feel when they are sad. You could help them write a poem themselves.

Make up a story

On pages 20–21 the stories have been broken down into four-stage sequences. Use this as a model to work together, making a simple sequence of events about somebody feeling sad and then feeling better. Ask your child to suggest the sequence of events and a way to resolve their story at the end.

An art session

Do a drawing session related to the feeling in this book. Here are some suggestions for drawings:

- A crying face.
- A laughing face.
- Chloe looking sad because she has lost Beebee.
- Omar happy with his new kittens.

An acting session

Choose a scene and act it out, for example:

- Role-play Chloe losing Beebee, feeling sad and telling her frends how she feels. Then act out her finding Beebee again with the help of her friends, and feeling better.
- Role-play Omar feeling sad about losing his cat, and then sharing happy memories with his Mum. Show Omar getting new kittens to look after, and feeling happier.